P9-BIX-715

Ranger's Pledge

I give my pledge as a member of
Ranger Rick's Nature Club

To use my eyes to see the
beauty of all outdoors;

To train my mind to learn
the importance of nature;

To use my hands to protect our air,
soil, water, woods and wildlife;

And by good example, to show
others how to respect,
properly use, and enjoy
our natural resources.

_____
Ranger's Name

Library of Congress Cataloging-in-Publication Data

Boyle, Doe.

Earth day every day / adapted by Doe Boyle ; illustrated by Cathy Beylon.
     p.   cm. — (Adventures of Ranger Rick)

Summary: Reluctant to help out on Earth Day, Boomer Badger is
convinced by his animal friends that there are many ways for individuals
to work to help keep the world clean.
     ISBN 0-924483-82-2
[1. Environmental protection — Fiction. 2. Earth day — Fiction.
3. Badgers — Fiction. 4. Animals — Fiction.]
I. Beylon, Cathy, ill. II. Ranger Rick. III. Ranger Rick. IV. Title. V. Series.
     PZ7.B69647Ear   1993   92-27292
     [E]—dc20   AC

From an original article (© National Wildlife Federation) which
appeared in _Ranger Rick_ magazine.
© National Wildlife Federation, 1993.

All rights reserved. No part of this book may be reproduced or
transmitted in any form or by any means whatsoever without prior
written permission of the publisher.

First Edition

10 9 8 7 6 5 4 3 2 1

Adventures of Ranger Rick storybooks are printed on paper which
includes a minimum of 10% post consumer waste.

Printed in Singapore.

Adventures of
Ranger Rick®
Earth Day Every Day

Adapted by Doe Boyle • Illustrated by Cathy Beylon

Soundprints

A Division of Trudy Management Corporation
Norwalk, Connecticut

One April morning, Becky Hare awoke to the sounds of bustling animals near her home in Deep Green Wood. She wriggled from her sleeping place and joined her friends under the old oak tree.

"I didn't know you were all so eager to begin our preparations for Earth Day," she said sleepily.

"Of course we are!" exclaimed Ranger Rick Raccoon. "Earth Day is a great time to teach people about the earth's needs. We can also show everyone what can be done to solve problems like air and water pollution. We got up early today to get ready for tomorrow's celebrations."

"Well, I'm glad you elected me to be leader of the festivities. Is everyone set to begin working?" asked Becky.

"I am! I am!" a chorus of voices answered. Rick, Ollie Otter, Cubby Bear, and Sammy Squirrel were as excited as Becky had ever seen them.

"I'm not," a grumbly voice muttered from behind the other animals. Boomer Badger pushed his way to the front of the crowd.

"Earth Day is a waste of time," he complained. "The Earth is a hopeless mess. People have ruined it — we'll never save it now."

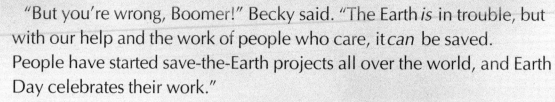

"But you're wrong, Boomer!" Becky said. "The Earth *is* in trouble, but with our help and the work of people who care, it *can* be saved. People have started save-the-Earth projects all over the world, and Earth Day celebrates their work."

"What kinds of projects?" Boomer asked grumpily.

"Come on — I'll show you some right here in Deep Green Wood," she said. Becky urged Boomer and all the animals to follow her along the path to Shady Pond.

Splashing and clanking sounds reached their ears as the animals arrived at the edge of Shady Pond. In the water Benny Bass was diving to find tin cans and other litter that had dropped to the bottom of the pond.

"Hi, everyone! Excuse me while I clean up for Earth Day," Benny hollered as he batted the cans onto the bank.

"See Boomer? Benny and others are keeping Shady Pond clean and clear, on Earth Day and every day. And look over here," Becky called as she walked along Clear Creek toward the meadow.

In the middle of the meadow Scarlett Fox tugged at a watering can. "Come see my Earth Day trees," she called.

On the ground around her were tiny potted trees. Scarlett had planted them in the cans that had littered the banks of Shady Pond.

"These tree seedlings are going to places that need trees," she explained. "Tomorrow we'll have an Earth Day planting along the old logging road. Soon it will be a green, shady lane."

"And that makes Deep Green Wood a healthier part of the planet," Becky told the animals.

Boomer began to look a little more cheerful. "How can we tell people what needs to be done next?" he asked.

"Follow me," Sammy Squirrel answered. "I'll show you."

The animals hiked back to the old oak tree, and Sammy scurried up the trunk to the hole that led to Ranger Rick's home. From the hole he pulled out posters he and Rick had painted to tell people how to care for the Earth.

"Boomer, people in thousands of places are pitching in just like us to make the Earth green and healthy again," Sammy chattered. "People are marching in big groups, carrying posters like these to ask folks to help save our planet. They're working to pass laws to clean the air and water. They're cleaning up beaches and streams, and they're working to save our forests, our flowers, and our animals. Everyone who pitches in makes a difference, and bad news changes to good news."

"Now I understand," Boomer said. "Earth Day is a celebration of work going on *every* day! Anyone who helps even in small ways makes the world a better place!"

"That's right," agreed Becky Hare, grinning at Boomer.

"Well, c'mon then — let's get started!" Boomer said happily. "What can I do?"

"Help me paint these shirts for our green parade tomorrow," said Ranger Rick.

"Help us scatter these wildflower seeds," chirped the songbirds in the trees.

"Help me clean up the trash near Clear Creek," called Ollie Otter.

"Wow! I have lots of ways to help the Earth today and celebrate Earth Day tomorrow!" Boomer exclaimed.

Becky Hare smiled at Boomer. "You sure have had a change of heart," she said.

"Well, folks like us are the heroes of Earth Day!" Boomer replied. "Our work means there's hope for the Earth and all its plants and animals. I can't sit around complaining and expecting someone else to do the job. Hey, Ollie — wait for me!" Boomer called, heading toward Clear Creek as Becky Hare painted a great green smile on her Earth Day poster.